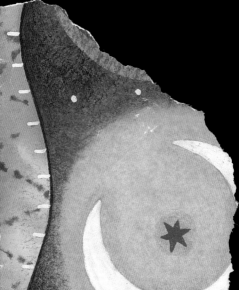

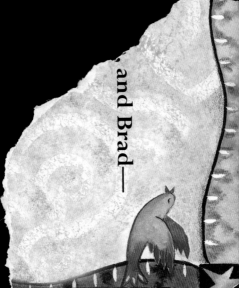

. and Brad—

Sing Praise

For Gary, Matt, Aaron, Lianna
with love.
—R. G. G.

For Tom, Aidan, and Finn
—J. B.

Large-quantity purchases or custom editions of this book are available at a discount from the publisher. For more information, contact the sales de partment at Augsburg Fortress, Publishers, 1-800-328-4648, or write to: Sales Director, Augsburg Fortress, Publishers, P. O. Box 1209, Minneapolis, MN 55440-1209.

The text is based on Psalm 148 and Psalm 150.

Library of Congress Cataloging-in-Publication Data
Greene, Rhonda Gowler.
Sing praise / by Rhonda Gowler Greene ; illustrated by Janet Broxon.
    p. cm.
Summary: In rhyming text and illustrations, all of nature, from animals and trees to the sun and moon and even the seasons, sing the praises of God.
ISBN 0-8066-5120-2 (pbk. : alk. paper)
[1. Nature—Fiction. 2. Christian life—Fiction. 3. Stories in rhyme.] I. Broxon, Janet, 1960- ill. II. Title.
    PZ8.3.G824Sin 2006
        [E]—dc22   2005010848

ISBN 0-8066-5120-2

Cover design by Diana Running
Book design by Sarah Olmanson and Michelle L. N. Cook

The paper used in this publication meets the minimum requirements of American National Standard for Information Sciences—Permanence of Paper for Printed Library Materials, ANSI Z329.48-1984. ⊗™

Manufactured in China.

09 08 07 06 05 1 2 3 4 5 6 7 8 9 10

This book belongs to

_____

From mouse to mighty elephant,
the animals sing praise.
Peeping, trilling, trumpeting,
their happy voices raise

a glad thanksgiving song to God,
   creator of them all,
who made the chanting chimpanzee,
   the buzzing bee, so small.

From oceans deep, sea creatures leap
and jump for joy in praise
and sing and play in salty spray
of splashing,
crashing waves

while on the air, the words of birds
weave merry melodies
that serenade with songs of praise
upon a carefree breeze.

Barn doves *coo* as milk cows *moo*
in beastly, joyful song.
Horses *n-ei-eigh* while donkeys *br-a-ay*
as piglets join along. *Oink!*

Frogs on logs hum *jug-a-rum*.
They praise with croaking calls
while rivers trickle, sing their songs
and rush in waterfalls.

Mountains, trees, stretch toward the sky,
majestic in their praise,
lifting songs from nature
days on days on days.

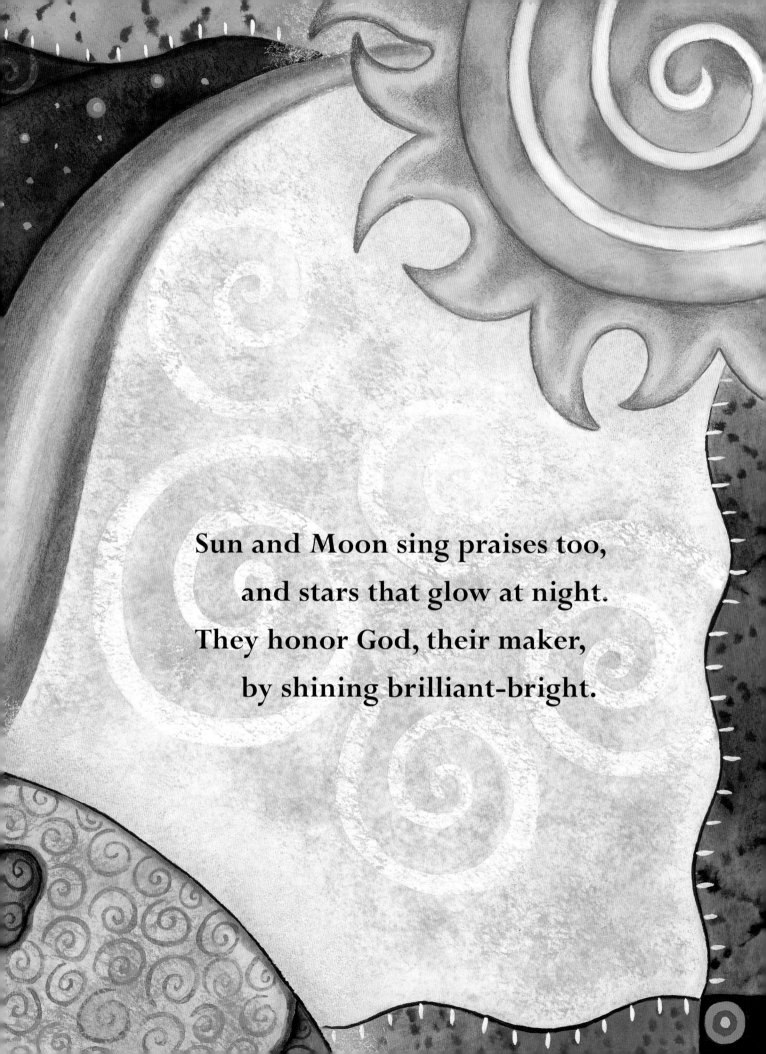

Sun and Moon sing praises too,
and stars that glow at night.
They honor God, their maker,
by shining brilliant-bright.

The seasons sing
     with wind and rain.
They whisper soft with snow.
Whirling round and round each year,
     God made them circle so.

The young, the old, proclaim their praise.
They open wide and sing
and play on instruments that chime
and clash
and clang
and ring.

With nimble feet,
they dance,
rejoice.

They swirl and twirl about
in grassy fields,
on busy streets,
in every town throughout.

All that breathe,

    the seasons round,

the stars and Moon, Sun's rays,

       rivers, trees, and mountains

    all sing a song of praise.

They raise up high
  in sweet refrain
    sincerest adoration,
praising God,
    exalting him . . .
      in song and celebration.